Fur BIDDEN

fur-ocious lust, book 1

New York Times and *USA Today* bestselling author
MILLY TAIDEN

This book is a work of fiction. The names, characters, places, and incidents are fictitious or have been used fictitiously, and are not to be construed as real in any way. Any resemblance to persons, living or dead, actual events, locales, or organizations is entirely coincidental.

Published By
Latin Goddess Press
New York, NY 10456
http://millytaiden.com
FUR-BIDDEN
Copyright © 2015 by Milly Taiden
Cover by Willsin Rowe
Formatting by Inkstain Interior Book Designing
All Rights Are Reserved. No part of this book may be used or reproduced in any manner whatsoever without written permission, except in the case of brief quotations embodied in critical articles and reviews.
Property of Milly Taiden 2015

fur-ocious lust, book 1

One

PENELOPE MEDINA DIDN'T know how to break the bad news to her best friends. Usually the go-to person to fix anything wrong, she was at a loss how to handle the situation. Karina and Julie chatted animatedly in the too-loud bar they always met at on Friday nights. The scent of smoke, liquor and cheap perfume filled the place. They weren't fond of the dive at first, but it turned into their favorite after-work hangout for the past year.

"So," she started, lifting an apple martini to her lips and taking a sip for courage. "I have something to tell you all."

Her friends stopped chatting about the latest issue at their non-profit and turned to her.

"Uh-oh," Kari said, picking up her cosmopolitan and taking a drink. "You look like you're about to give us bad news."

She was. Dammit! Why did she have to be the one to do it? Jerk-off Dave should be doing it. Not her. She hadn't signed them up for anything. Dave had, but somehow Penny was the one stuck delivering the bad news.

"Please don't hate me."

"Whoa!" Julie stopped her. "I can already tell I'm not going to like whatever you're going to say, so hang on a sec." She motioned for a refill on her glass of sangria and once that had been taken care of, she gulped the thing down. She then placed it on the table and smacked her lips. "Okay, hit me."

"I swear, Julie, one of these days you're going to fall flat on your face when you stand after doing that a few times. I don't know how you can handle that." Kari laughed.

"Dave signed us up for the bachelorette auction on Sunday," Penny blurted out. Taking a note from Julie, she gulped the rest of her martini. She winced at the burning liquid going down her throat. She had never done that. Not really a drinker, she tended to nuzzle her glass for hours. Tonight called for drastic measures.

"What do you mean he signed *us* up?" Kari screeched.

Yeah. That's the reaction she'd been waiting for. They were three very big girls working for the largest wildlife conservation non-profit in the state. They signed on to work for the company because they loved animals, not to be on a stage getting sold like pieces of meat.

"Penny, I hate to break this to you, but we're shy big girls with bad attitudes," Kari said, her brown eyes wide with surprise.

"Yeah, not just big, we're short. We're not model material. We don't even have the personalities to be good dates." Julie blinked, picking up her glass again and motioning for another refill. "I don't think bitchy goes well with anything."

"I know all of this. Quite frankly, I'm probably more surprised than you two that Dave did that. He knows how we feel about being in the spotlight." She sighed. "But he said we are the best at fundraising and his wife suggested we fill the three empty slots left on the list."

"Weren't all the spots filled?" Kari asked.

"Yeah, but there was a disagreement with some of the volunteers. Apparently, Dave asked them to get clothes they didn't feel comfortable in. He told them to 'sex it up' because 'sex sells' and it would bring the auction lots of money."

"What a douche." Julie shook her head. "So now that leaves us parading on a stage and hoping some poor sap buys us or looking pathetic in front of the entire place, but no pressure, huh?"

None at all.

"We can always quit," Kari suggested, her shoulders slumping. "I don't want to quit though. I love my job."

"Yeah, I do too," Julie said, tossing a long strand of jet-black hair over her shoulder. "Who knew we'd be so good at asking people for money."

Penny curled her fingers over her lap. She hated that Dave had put them in such an uncomfortable position.

Two years ago, Penny had started working at Soaring for Wildlife. Months later, she had met a man she had fallen hard and fast for. The same could be said of her friends. The men were all brothers. But lies, lack of communication, and deception had torn their relationships apart.

Twinges of sadness pinched at her heart. Why did she choose that moment to think of Ethan? Their relationship had lasted only a few months. It'd been filled with lust, romance and half-truths. In the end, that's what killed it. She refused to ask him about things he should have felt comfortable sharing with her. Personal things.

"Look..." She bit her lip, pushing away the memories of Ethan and his blue eyes. "We can say no, but he made it clear our jobs were on the line."

"He's bluffing," Julie said. "We're the best he's got."

"Yeah. Why would he want to get rid of us when we get him more donations between the three of us than everyone in that office, combined?" Kari asked.

The waitress took their empty glasses and brought them fresh drinks. They never had more than one or two, but it appeared tonight was going to be a "walking home" kind of night.

"He's not bluffing." She hated having to give more bad news to her friends. "He showed me three resumes of candidates that come from very well-off backgrounds willing to pull strings to bring the type of donations we have only dreamed of."

"Shit," Julie growled. "This is fucked up. Real fucked up."

"Let me just have five minutes alone with Dave and I will rearrange his face," Kari promised.

"Nobody is getting arrested. We're just going to have to…do it."

Julie made a face of disgust, scrunching her nose and pursing her lips. "Fine. But if neither of you kick Dave in the balls if nobody buys us, I will."

Penny had a plan for that. "That's not going to happen." At least there was something she could do to help them all out in the auction. "I've asked my assistant, Charlie, to buy the three of us. I'm giving him money to at least make it look good."

"I'll double it!" Kari grinned. "I don't want to be sold too cheaply."

"Oh, brother." Julie shook her head.

"Whatever. You know you're going to do the same thing." Kari raised her brows at Julie.

A grin spread over Julie's lips. "Yeah, she's right. Screw Dave. I'll just make my yearly donation work for me."

Great. Now all they needed was for their plan to work, and for Charlie not to leave them hanging.

Two

ETHAN SINCLAIR TURNED away from his office window to face the door. His brothers had just walked in. The three bear shifters owned the largest home-building company in the country, Sinclair Building Co..

"Why did you call us?" Rafe asked. Though they were triplets, identical physically, they were completely different in personalities. Ethan was the one behind the contracts. He interfaced with clients and other contractors on a daily basis. Rafe handled builders and materials. Then there was Ash. He was their company's PR man. He helped create their brand and launch Sinclair to the next level. Now they were three of the most powerful men in the United States. All thanks to their exes.

"Penelope, Julie and Karina." He didn't bother warming them up.

"What about them?" Rafe asked, shoving his hands in his pockets and clenching his jaw. He hated talking about Julie.

Ash didn't say a word. He just stood there, his arms folded over his white dress shirt.

"Fine. I can see this is not going to be easy so I'll make it simple. Ash knows we are big donors to the Soaring for Wildlife non-profit. I've made it my business that we donate anonymously every year but the director, Theo, is a friend of mine. He's a lion-shifter who is grateful for our help."

"Get to the point," Rafe growled.

"Fine. The point is that all three of them work at Soaring and we have a chance, if you want to take it, to possibly rectify the situation with them."

Ash lifted a brow. "How?"

"We are the main sponsors for their bachelorette auction this weekend. Theo managed to get the three of them on the roster to be auctioned off for a date. That means you get one chance to ensure your mates listen to you. One chance to change the fuck-ups from the past." Shit. Saying it out loud sounded even more ominous. He wanted Penny, but she'd hung up on every call he made. She'd ignored his visits and had gone as far as changing her number. Yeah, he'd fucked up big time. This was his chance to get her back. A year without her had been worse than any hell. He'd been waiting for the opportunity to find his way back into her life and he knew that his brothers felt the same way about their women. "Let's just say tonight, they have no choice but to talk to us. I set this up and I ensured Theo would make things happen."

Rafe marched forward, his frame stiffening with every step. "There's no guarantee this will work. They can refuse to see us. Or leave with us."

Ethan grinned. "I have a plan." He pressed a button on his phone and spoke. "Kyle, get in here."

His assistant, Kyle, was a young bear with the ability to smooth talk his way into anything.

Kyle flung the door open and eyed the three men before breaking into a grin. "You told them I'm buying their women?"

Rafe made a deep growling noise in his chest. "Be careful kid. Don't want to break your face. That's the only thing you got going for you."

"I'll have you know, I have the plan all worked out. All you have to do is be at your assigned spot." Kyle puffed out his chest. "You don't pay me the big bucks for nothing."

"Isn't he an intern?" Ash asked.

Ethan laughed. "Yeah."

"Alright," Kyle conceded. "You don't pay me, but once this mission is over, I expect a raise and a bonus and possibly even a vacation."

"You can expect your ass kicked if it doesn't go well," Ash said.

"Such violence!" Kyle grumbled.

"We're fucking bears. What did you expect, sweet talking and roses?" Rafe snapped.

"See that..." Kyle pointed at Rafe while staring at Ethan. "That's why Julie left his ass. I can't promise she'll take him back, Ethan. I'm not a miracle worker. Besides, what if she likes me?"

"Oh, brother," Ash groaned.

Rafe took a step towards Kyle. "I'm gonna—"

"Rafe, stop!" Ethan ordered. "He's going to help and you're going to let him. Now give them both the information they need to be at the right place at the right time, Kyle."

"Fine," Rafe said. "You get to live another day kid."

"You know..." Kyle took slow steps backward. "If I didn't know better I would swear you have not smiled since you and Julie broke up."

"I think you need another plan, Ethan. I'm killing the kid," Rafe said.

Kyle shot out of the room in a heartbeat. He wasn't stupid. Rafe was almost twice his size. All three of them were.

"So what do you think of the plan?" Ethan asked his brothers.

"I think it can work." Ash nodded. "Even if we only get the one chance to talk to them."

"We should come clean already. They didn't deserve the lies." Ethan gripped his pen hard. He wanted to be with Penny. He'd hated letting her go when she'd realized he was keeping things from her. Now, he wasn't going to let another year filled with torture, because he missed her, go by.

"I'm not so sure the truth will be enough with Julie." Rafe marched to the bar at the right side of Ethan's office. He poured three drinks and handed one to each Ash and Ethan.

"Do whatever you need to, to get your woman back, Rafe. Unless you want to keep living without her."

Three

PENNY GLANCED AT the sexiest dress she owned on the backstage mirror. It was a sapphire-blue strapless that showed off her large chest but fell in a cascade of silk, accentuating her curves. It was the first dress she'd bought after leaving Ethan with the thought of dating again, so many months after leaving Ethan. She'd never worn it. Not once. Oh well, it would have to do. It wasn't like she ever went on a date. In fact, she hadn't dated at all since she'd been with him. Ethan had messed her up for all men. His looks. His kisses. He'd been the best for her and she wasn't interested in comparing anyone to him. Besides, she still loved him. There was no way she could honestly feel right about having sex with anyone else when she still wanted the jerk.

Her turn was coming up on the stage. She shoved the curtain to the side, checking out the tables full of couples already getting to know each other. Maybe they'd stop things short and she could be saved.

"There you are!"

She whirled around to face Dave and his wife. Normally, she only disliked Dave, but at that moment she hated his wife, too. Still, she nodded at the woman who gave her what appeared to be a sincere smile. "You look great, Penny."

"Thanks." She managed to get the words out past the lump in her throat. She hated being on-stage. It was why her job was so perfect. All she did was call people. Go to lunch with a single person in charge of charitable contributions. There were no big meetings or public speaking engagements. Her heart started pumping faster than ever.

"You're on, Penny!" she heard someone say.

Holy crap. She couldn't move. Stage fright was going to kill her and she wasn't even on stage yet.

"Come on, darling." Dave's wife, Meredith guided her towards the stage. "Nothing to be afraid of. You're doing something wonderful for charity."

Right. Charity. She needed to keep reminding herself of that or she might throw up. And how sexy would *that* look?

The curtains opened and everyone started clapping. To her right, the Director of Soaring Wildlife stood at a podium and spoke into a mic.

"Now we have the lovely Ms. Penelope Medina."

She glanced out at the crowd but was having a hard time seeing the people with the lights right in her face. She didn't walk up and down like the others had, instead she stood at the same spot, like a petrified animal.

"Ms. Medina is one of our best Development Managers. She likes to dance to eighties freestyle when no one is watching, and she sings in the shower," he read from a paper.

She almost broke her neck jerking around to stare at the director. Who the hell told him that about her? Laughter broke out across the room.

"Ms. Medina is also a fan of Tom and Jerry cartoons and her favorite ice cream is anything with chocolate, vanilla and caramel mixed together. Now let's open up the bid for a night on the town with Ms. Medina. Do I hear fifty dollars?"

Penny couldn't believe someone had divulged her personal information for the stupid auction. The worst part was that she knew it wasn't Dave. He wasn't that familiar with her. She immediately dismissed her friends. She had enough dirt to bury them both. So, who did it?

She heard her assistant, Charlie, yell. "One hundred dollars!"

"I have one hundred dollars from number thirty-five. Do I hear one-fifty?" said the director.

Things were going according to plan. For a second, she thought no other bids were going to come in and smiled, thinking the worst of the night almost over.

"Two hundred dollars," a new voice yelled.

Crap. She squinted into the crowd, trying to find the person bidding against Charlie.

"I have two hundred from the gentleman by the bar," the director said.

Her gaze roamed to the farthest area in the back of the room and she saw a slim young man standing there. She couldn't make out his features well enough to know if she knew him. Fucking hell.

"Two-fifty!" Charlie threw in.

"Three hundred," said the slim guy.

"Three-fifty," yelled Charlie.

She'd only given Charlie five hundred thinking for sure it wouldn't go that high. Now she worried he would lose and soon.

"Four hundred," said the slim guy again, getting ahead of Charlie.

"Five hundred." That was Charlie's highest bid. She held her breath, waiting to see if the other guy would top it.

"I have five hundred from number thirty-five. Do I hear six?" The director encouraged the crowd.

Silence.

"Five hundred dollars going once. Going twice—"

"Fifty thousand dollars," yelled the slim guy.

A murmur rippled through the crowd. She must have heard wrong. The murmur grew louder.

Ah, fuck! She hadn't heard wrong. Why would he pay fifty thousand dollars for dinner with her? What type of person had that kind of money to throw away?

"Fifty thousand going once. Going twice. Sold to the gentleman by the bar for a fifty thousand-dollar donation to Soaring Wildlife. Please meet Ms. Medina by our payment area and we will gladly send you on your way."

Four

THE CROWD WENT wild cheering for the highest donation of the night so far. Penny's stomach rolled, sending bile shooting up her throat. She could only hope her night got better.

She turned around to go back through the curtain, her hands shaking and her muscles so stiff she swore they'd break. Breathe. She needed to breathe. Spots danced before her eyes.

"Holy shit, Penny!" Julie gasped, clutching her by the shoulders. "You look like you're going to faint."

Penny gasped for air, her lungs burning with panic.

"Breathe, Penny," Kari said softly. "You'll be fine. The guy didn't appear to be more than a kid. Maybe he fell in love at first sight?" She giggled. "Who knows?"

Good. Okay. Why was she freaking out? Oh yeah, the whole time on stage had really messed her up. She took deep breaths, trying to calm the racing in her heart. She wasn't a fan of stages. Or crowds.

Soft as marshmallows, her legs shook with each step she took. "I'm fine. Really, guys. I'm okay."

She cleared her throat and glanced around, looking for the payment area. Where was Dave, that asshole?

"Hey, I wouldn't be so pissed if some young kid bought me," Julie muttered, letting go of Penny's arm. "At least, that would be easier to digest than the looks on some of these old guys' faces."

Penny saw what Julie meant. There were some old men giving bachelorettes lecherous looks and smiling at them like they were pimp daddies. "You're right. This can't be so bad. He's a kid."

A burst of confidence went through her, calming her nerves. This wasn't such a big deal. This was for charity. Why was she getting so worked up? Besides, how many times had she done this before? None. So her worst fears could be unfounded.

"Our next lady up for bid..."

"Crap!" Kari groaned. "My turn. This sucks balls."

"Good luck, girls," Penny said, glancing back at the dreaded stage. "I'll see you all Monday."

"Have fun tonight." Julie smiled. Her sparkling brown eyes filled with concern. "Don't stress so much. This is supposed to be fun all around."

She nodded and marched, with steadier steps, toward the area her friends said was the payment section.

The young man she'd seen from the stage waited for her with a wide smile on his face. He was young, probably early twenties or late teens. "Hi, I'm Kyle."

She shook his hand and immediately felt more at ease. From his short dark hair to his slim frame, the guy didn't give off any jerk vibes. His smile was genuine, which helped her calm down. "Hi. I'm Penelope, but everyone calls me Penny."

"I like that name. Penny. Are you one of the lucky ones?" he asked, the smile growing wider.

She laughed at the question she got from almost everyone. "I like to think so. Did you have something in mind you wanted to do tonight?"

He nodded and offered her his arm. "My car is waiting outside. I think you'll like the place I found for dinner."

She cleared her throat, pushing back the renewed nerves. She didn't normally go anywhere with strangers. Even a young one. Taking his arm, she strolled out of the hall with Kyle. She'd never done a bachelorette auction before so she wasn't sure what the plan was. Thanks to idiot Dave, she hadn't even been filled in on the process.

A shiny black stretch limo sat at the curve of the hotel. Kyle waved at the driver, telling him to stay in place and opened a door for her. She entered the limo and the door closed behind her. A quick glance around made her breath seize in her lungs.

"Ethan?"

The limo sped off and she barely managed to sit properly before she would have fallen on her face. She glanced around, noting that Kyle never got in the limo. Her gaze ate up the man she'd loved but let go.

He'd always worn his brown hair in a shaggy cut that didn't appear to be tamed. His aqua-blue eyes pinned her with a commanding stare. "You look beautiful, Penny."

"What the hell are you doing here?" she screeched in outrage then gasped. "You set this up. You asshole!"

Her chest ached from how good it was to see him and how much it hurt at the same time. She'd missed him so much, but she refused to be with a liar. She didn't care how much he said he loved her. If he truly did, he wouldn't have lied about some really big things in their relationship, things she expected to know under any circumstance. From the fact he had money down to his species. All of it had been lies.

He leaned forward, his tux shifting with his moves. Christ he had such a big body. She'd always loved that about him. He wasn't all muscle either. He had a well-defined body with strength. It was probably all part of being a bear-shifter. She'd fallen so hard for Ethan. Her mind still couldn't wrap around the fact that he'd kept so much from her. All the while claiming to love her.

"Let me out of this car!" She turned to face the closed partition between them and the driver. Wiggling and sliding down the long curved seat, she was about to knock on the glass when Ethan grabbed her arm, turning her to face him.

"Penny, listen to me."

The limo took a sharp turn and she fell back with Ethan sprawled over her.

"Get off me!" She tried to push him off, but he was too big and strong. He pinned her down until she couldn't move and she wasn't a small woman. She had boundless curves and weight on her body.

She huffed out an angry breath and glared at him. "I don't care how much you paid, I'll have them refund your donation. Now let me out because I am not going anywhere with you."

He held her hands above her head on the seat with one hand and grabbed her chin, forcing her to meet his gaze with the other.

"That's enough!" he roared.

Five

SHE BLINKED, HER heart thundering wildly. She'd never seen him get so angry before.

"Stop acting like a spoiled brat, Penelope." His breath caressed her face and the hint of mint and whiskey floated up her nose. "I wouldn't have had to do this if you would have answered my damn calls. Or opened the door and talked to me."

"You lied to me! I hate liars."

"You don't hate me, babe. You love me," he threw back.

She growled and tried to free herself again. "You are a dick. A big dick."

"I have a big dick. One that's been missing you like crazy, Penny. Stop!" He growled again. "All that moving is only making me want to rip this fucking dress off and fuck you right here right now."

She gasped. "You think I'd let you touch me after what you did?"

He clenched his jaw tight. "What did I do that was so wrong? Keep my finances to myself?"

She rolled her eyes and huffed another growl. "You never told me you were a bear!"

His hand on her face kept her from glancing away from his too-knowing eyes. "You have a problem with me being a shifter?"

"No, you asshole. I have a problem with not being told things that I should know. Like the fact you can turn into a big-ass bear. That's my problem. Get it yet?"

"What the hell does that have to do with anything? If you love me, like you said you did, then you wouldn't care about any of that."

She squirmed again and stopped the moment she felt his erection pressing between her legs. Fucking hell. Now was not the time to get excited he was hard. "I did love you. I didn't care that you were a shifter, but I cared about the lack of trust. You could have told me. It wouldn't have made a difference. I cared about you for you."

"You still love me. Don't fucking try to deny what I can see in your eyes." He rocked his hips between her legs, rubbing his erection right on her clit.

A soft gasp escaped her throat and she bit her lip to keep from moaning. "I can't love a liar."

"I never lied to you." His fierce gaze didn't budge. "I told you I loved you and I was honest."

She glanced down at his lips, her breaths coming in short shallow bursts. "If you loved me, you would have trusted me. Told me about your ass being loaded and a shifter. But you didn't trust me! Get off me!"

He growled and instead of moving like she wanted, he brought his head down and plastered his lips over hers in an angry, soul-sucking kiss that took her breath away. She didn't want to want him. Didn't want to love him. But her body refused to listen. The kiss set off detonations of hunger exploding through her veins. She breathed through his lips, sharing his air and letting him possess her once again. He rubbed his tongue over hers, twirling and sucking and making her lose all control. Pleasure intensified with each swipe of his tongue on her lips.

Every nip and nibble sent a stream of wetness down her pussy.

He tore his lips from hers and inhaled a short, harsh breath. "You want me."

She licked her lips, still staring at his too-sexy mouth and lied. "I don't."

"You're so fucking wet for me, Penny."

"Bullshit. You have a good imagination." She refused to admit defeat. She didn't care how much her body burned for the bear. She wouldn't give in to her hormones.

"Bullshit?" He lowered his head again, sucking on her chin and licking her jaw. "I know I make you wet. I bet if I shove my hand between your legs you'll be fucking soaked."

She swallowed back a whimper. Lord have mercy on her soul. "You're delusional. I don't want you."

"You can lie to yourself, but you can't lie to me. Your body aches for me to get inside you. Your pussy throbs for a taste of my cock."

Holy shit. Hearing him say it only made her wetter. "I don't know what you're talking about. I know how to control myself."

"You're a piece of work. You lay there, wet and horny as fuck, wanting me to fuck you every way possible and you refuse to admit it."

She licked her lips and raised her brows. "Let me out of this car. I don't negotiate with liars."

"I'm not a liar!" He took her mouth again, this time even harder than before. The sound of material tearing resonated in the back of her mind, but the way he fucked her mouth with his tongue pushed it all away. She gave in, just a little, and kissed him as hard as he kissed her. A loud rumble sounded from his chest, making her entire body vibrate.

Then his mouth was on her neck, sucking, biting, driving her crazy with each touch. She couldn't look down; he still had a hand on her face, holding it in place. It took a second to realize he wasn't holding her hands above her head any longer. He'd released them and she'd kept them up there on her own.

She gripped his hair in her fist. At first, to pull him away, but the moment his lips sucked on her nipple it changed to keep him there. She hated how badly she wanted him. It had always been like this between them. Hot. Rough. Dangerous.

Her temperature shot to the moon when he nipped at her breast. It was so good. So right. He slid his hand down her body and between her legs, yanking at the material of her panties. The bite of pain from the pull of the silk didn't faze her. She ignored that and opened wide. Maybe for this one time she could take what he offered. A quick bout of pleasure before she sent him away from her. There wasn't going to be a relationship between them again. But this, sex, she could do.

He groaned on her breast and released her nipple. He pressed his palm on her pussy, pushing his fingers into her entrance. "Fuck, Penny. I told you you'd be wet."

She gulped and tried to push her need for more of his touch away. "I'm not."

His face came into view. The angry frown and the way he pressed his lips into a thin line made her heart flip-flop. "Now who's the liar?" He spread her pussy lips wide open and flicked a finger on her clit. "You don't want to want me, but you do. You're fucking visualizing me up in your pussy. Deny it all you want, but my cock is the only one that does this to you. I make you slick. I make you hot. I make you come." His finger circled the sensitive nub and she moaned. "Say it. Say you want me to fuck you."

"I—"

He fingered her pussy, drawing out a low moan from her. "Say you want my dick inside you. You know you do. You've been thinking about it since the last time I fucked you."

She gasped, closing her eyes and then opening them again to his piercing gaze. "Ethan..."

"That's it baby," he said when she grew slicker. "You remember that last time. It was kind of like this. In a limo. Remember how I ate your pussy until you gushed on my face?"

Oh, good god how could she ever forget that. It had been unreal. She nodded, her body trying to take the tenuous control out of her grasp.

"You wet my face with your juices and then I kissed you. You tasted yourself on my mouth and begged me to fuck you. Remember that, sweetheart? Remember my cock deep in your pussy?" He pushed two fingers into her and drew them out slowly. "You moaning how much you liked it. Your nails digging my back and your legs spread wide so I could go deeper and deeper." His fingers went in and out of her faster, picking up speed with his words. "I remember. Maybe it's time I reminded you how much your pussy likes my cock sliding in and out of you. How much you love me coming inside you, leaving you sticky and wet and then eating you out all over again."

Fucking hell! Why did he do that to her? "Ethan, I can't—"

He brushed his lips lightly over hers. "Say it. You want to. I know because I haven't wanted another like I want you. I haven't been with anyone since you. And there will not be any others. It's just you."

She didn't know if he was lying or telling the truth, but those words did something to her. It opened the door she'd shut a year ago and emotions poured out of her like a glass of wine overflowing. "Please." She swallowed. "I've missed you."

That's all it took. He pushed the frothy skirt out of the way and unzipped. His gaze was stuck to hers. There was no need for further workup or words. All she wanted was him. Inside her. Taking her. Being hers. He pushed the head of his cock into her slick channel with a single-minded thrust and didn't stop until he was balls deep inside her, until she was choking for a breath from her body was trying to adjust to being taken after almost a year without him.

"Fuck, baby. You're still just as perfect as before." He pulled his hips back and pressed forward with determined drives.

She clawed at his suit jacket, wishing the damn thing was off him, but not wanting to stop him for anything. He fucked her the way she loved. Hard. Fast. Deep. So deep. Until they were pelvis to pelvis with no space between them.

"Yes..." she moaned.

The limo hit a bump and his thrust felt deeper. She didn't care that his hand was still on her neck, holding her in place. She only focused on the pleasure of his body going in and out of hers. Tension mounted inside her, curling at the pit of her belly into a ball, ready to unfurl at any second.

"Lord, you feel good." He sucked on the corner of her mouth, biting his way down to her neck. "Your pussy's so tight. So wet. I've been dreaming of being inside you again for the past year." He drew circles over her skin with his tongue. "Dreams of coming in your pussy. In your mouth. Taking you every way. You'd let me. You'd want me to fuck you hard and rough until your legs were useless."

She moaned, her lungs burning from the lack of air. She visualized him doing even more to her. Just like he had in the past. "Yes, I would let you."

"I know," he groaned, his words coming out choppy and strained. "You loved it when I fucked you from behind and yanked on your gorgeous hair. And when I slapped your ass. Didn't you, Penny?"

She did. Dammit all to hell she did! She'd never wanted a man to do any of that to her until Ethan. He'd opened her up to want things she'd never thought sexy. He'd done stuff to her she hadn't even thought of. "I—"

"Don't deny it now, love," he rumbled. "I've licked and fucked you in every way possible. I've loved watching you play with yourself when you sucked my dick. Fuck! That was so sexy." He thrust harder, his moves almost losing their precision.

"Ethan," she gasped. Her muscles stiffened. She was so close. So close to jumping off the cliff and diving into a whirlpool of pleasure. "I'm so..."

"I got you, beautiful." He lowered his head to her chest and bit down on her nipple. Sucking and biting hard and fucking her with the same aggression did the trick. His pelvis rubbed on her clit, adding just the right amount of friction to push her over the edge and send her soaring.

She screamed, clutching on-to his jacket and taking a pounding from his cock at the same time her pussy contracted around him with her orgasm. She slid up and down on the leather seat, her back slick with sweat. Then he stiffened, groaning and pumping with a speed she knew meant he was closing in on his own release. Once. Twice. He stopped, bit harder on her tit and groaned. His cock pulsed in her pussy, filling her with his seed.

Six

ETHAN HELD THE woman he'd fallen for like a stone in his arms. Two years ago, he'd broken all the rules his family had lived with and started dating Penny. She was a human, unlike any of the females in his clan. At first, he'd chosen not to tell her about his shifter status because he wasn't sure how she'd react. Not that he hadn't slept with human females, but she was different. She was the one. The more time he spent with her, the more he realized he didn't want her to leave him. Unlike him and his brothers, she'd been raised dirt poor with almost nothing to her name.

Thinking of her history and how she'd come out of it, the struggle she'd endured to become something in a family of nothing, tugged at his heart. He'd been trying to figure out how to tell her of his wealth without sounding full of himself. Or without making her feel like she wasn't good enough for him.

What ended up happening, was that she'd found out through word of mouth, something he hadn't expected. He could almost hear her brain working, trying to decide what to do about him. About them. Only this time, he wouldn't let her just close him out and push him away because she felt deceived. He'd never actually lied to her. He'd gone as far as baring his soul so she could see he loved her. Nothing had worked.

"Ethan." She shifted, leaving his arms, holding with one hand the pieces of what used to be her dress up to her chest. She slipped shaky fingers through her curls, pushing the long, dark strands away from her face. "We need to talk."

He didn't dare smile, though he wanted to, at the mussed-up hair and smeared make-up. God, she was so fucking beautiful. Even like this: angry, confused and a mess, he wanted her again. She could be wearing a box and he'd want her. There was no taming the desire he felt for her. Would always feel for her.

He handed her his shirt, hoping she'd feel more comfortable wearing that, but also for his own peace of mind. There was no way in hell he'd be able to sit there and talk to her when all he wanted to do was tear the fabric away and fuck her until he came inside her at least three more times. He wanted to pound her hard, fucking her until he couldn't go on, draining himself in her. The bear demanded he reclaim her body.

"I never lied to you," he said. Though saying the words he'd repeated to her should be easy, it still bothered him that she had honestly believed him capable of deceit. He might not have told her about his bear or his money, but he never lied about his feeling for her. Ever.

"Look." She cleared her throat, her gaze sweeping down his naked torso and his pants' open fly. "I don't know if I could trust you after that."

He stayed where he was. The bear snarled and huffed, wanting to get her to understand she belonged with him. "You love me."

She narrowed her eyes, pursed her lips and took a slow breath. "Love is not the issue here. Trust is."

"I never lied about my feeling for you. I love you. I have since the first moment I saw you. I love everything about you." He stared her down, holding her gaze captive and willing her to believe him. "I love your attitude. I love your sexy-as-hell body. All those curves make me fucking crazy. I love your generosity in wanting to work saving wild life. I love the fact that you have been offered jobs that pay more and refuse them to stay at a non-profit."

Her eyes widened. "Who told you about that?"

He shrugged. "I know everything about you, love. I've never for a second stopped thinking about you. About bringing you back to where you belong, with me."

She bit her lip and frowned. "Why didn't you tell me about your money? Or the fact you were a shifter?"

"You were so open about having nothing most of your life. I hated that I'd grown up with none of those problems. I tried to not sound like a jackass by flaunting money or suggesting things that would make you uncomfortable."

"I don't understand."

He smiled. He'd paid attention to her. He'd seen her reaction when he'd given her some inexpensive gifts and how she'd almost refused them. "I had to stop myself from giving you everything I saw, because you made it clear that buying you things was not the way to get your attention."

She nodded. "It's not. I don't need material things. I've done without them and can continue to. That's not what makes me happy."

He took a deep breath, his stomach burning from the words that were ready to spill. "I was scared to lose you. I thought if you knew I had money, you'd push me away."

"I—"

"I shouldn't have kept that from you. I thought that if you didn't find out until later on, things would be easier for you to get used to."

"I loved you, Ethan. I would have understood. Just because I didn't have money doesn't mean I'd begrudge you yours. That's selfish and wrong."

He laughed dryly. "I see that now."

"What about the other thing? Why not explain to me about your bear? Did you think I didn't know about shifters?"

"No. It wasn't that. Many women get caught up in the idea of being with a shifter and they either freak out, thinking we're going to somehow hurt them, or they start asking for strange things."

"Again. You didn't trust me enough to tell me. You thought I would be like the others."

"At first I didn't know you well enough."

"But after?"

"I was wrong. I...I should have told you but by then, you were entrenched in my heart. In my blood. I couldn't imagine you not being in my life." He opened himself up, ready for the possibility of her rejection but still willing to let her know how he felt. "You're the first woman I have cared enough about that it worried me what you thought."

"Take me home, Ethan. I need to think." She bit her lip and glanced away. "I'm not saying I don't want to see you again. I just need to figure out if I can be in a relationship with you and trust you. If I can't, then there is no saying yes to you. It would be a waste of both our time. The last thing either one of us needs is a relationship with no trust."

He nodded, willing to give her the time and space she needed. Only he wasn't just going to go away. He wasn't going to disappear into the night and pretend he didn't love her, that he didn't want her. A year without her had been hell and he wasn't going to go through another.

He pressed the intercom button and gave the driver her address. His mind worked out the plans for getting her back in his life again. Money was no longer an issue; he'd use whatever means necessary to show her he loved her, to show her how much he cared.

When they reached her house, he got out of the limo and helped her to her front door. She wrapped his shirt around her, so big it looked like a dress on her.

She opened her door and turned to face him, her eyes filled with confusion. "Thank you for bringing me back. And for the donation."

He nodded, watching her get ready to close the door on him. The bear didn't want to let go just yet. He shoved his foot in the door and pushed it wide enough to fit his frame. She opened her mouth to say something but he hooked a hand around her neck and pulled her to him. He brought his lips down over hers. The sound of her soft moan drove the beast forward.

A rumble sounded in his chest. He yanked the bear back, focusing his energy on the taming of her lips. The sweet taste of her appeased some of his hunger, but not enough. The soft whimpers of pleasure turned his hard cock concrete stiff. He needed inside her again. Fuck fuck fuck! All he wanted was to lay her down and eat her pussy and drive his cock so deep her pussy would clasp around him. She'd moan and offer her tits to him and he'd take her all fucking night. That's what he wanted. For the rest of his damn life.

He yanked away from the temptation she'd become and met her stunned gaze. He licked his lips, taking in the lingering flavor. How he wanted to lick her smooth caramel skin all over, to kiss his way down her spine until he reached her ass and dipped his tongue between her cheeks. She puffed out a breath and tortured her bottom lip with her teeth.

"Don't tempt me anymore," he growled. "All I want to do right now is fuck you against this door."

Her brows rose and her lips lifted in a small grin. "I don't think you sound like someone who has his beast under control."

He glanced at the slightly open neckline of his shirt, showing off her mouth-watering tits. "My beast wants to fuck you. I want to fuck you. And to be honest with you, I could probably spend the rest of my life with you, in a bed, your legs spread wide, sating my hunger for you."

She glanced over his shoulder. "Let me think, Ethan."

"You've had a year to think, Penny. It's my turn to make you mine again."

She gulped and the scent of her arousal tickled his bear. She was going to drive him fucking crazy. He could tell she liked that he was half out of his mind wanting her. His brother Rafe was right, women were a lot of work. He thought about Penny under him, screaming his name and decided the reward of having her back was worth it though.

He turned around and marched to the limo, the bear snapping at his heels and begging to be let loose.

Seven

ETHAN'S INSTINCT WAS to grab the largest bouquet of tulips he could find. He knew those were Penny's favorite, and he planned to make sure she knew he was going to get her back. It wasn't a matter of if; it was a matter of when. She would be his again. Fuck that, she was his, she just needed to remember.

He knew it was early and she'd probably be at home, puttering around like she tended to do on a Saturday morning when she didn't have to go anywhere. He'd found out all about her schedule and knew this was the day she stayed home and relaxed.

He rung her bell and waited, excitement roaring inside him in the form of an antsy bear. He wanted to see her. If it were up to his animal, he'd never be away from her. Though most of his clan liked to live solitary lives, when they found a mate, there was no being away from them. Ethan had seen the change in himself the moment he met Penny. There were no longer thoughts of being away from the world. Everything revolved around her and making her happy. For months, that's exactly how it had gone.

The door swung open and Penny stood in doorway, her nose red and her eyes watery.

"What happened? You looked fine last night." He marched inside, ignoring the fact she hadn't invited him in.

"Gee, thanks." She sniffled and sneezed. "I've been working hard and had the sniffles recently. It's turned into a full-blown cold."

Panic coursed through him, seizing his ability to breathe. Penny had never gotten sick when they were together before. He wanted to make her feel better. He had to do something to help her.

He shoved the flowers into her hands. "What can I get you?"

She glanced down at the bouquet of tulips and then lifted her shiny gaze to his. "These are so beautiful."

"Never mind the flowers." He urged her toward the sofa, dropping his cell phone on the coffee table in front of her. "Lay down."

She blinked up at him, her stunned gaze going from the flowers to him. "I'm not going to fall over because I have a cold. What are you doing here anyway?"

He took the flowers out of her hands and headed for her kitchen. He'd learned the layout well enough back when they'd dated. He searched her cupboards until he found an empty glass vase and half-filled it with water before arranging the flowers. "I wanted to ask if you wanted to go for breakfast."

She sneezed again. He brought the vase to the coffee table and put them where she could look at the tulips.

"I don't really feel like going out." She coughed. "I'm kind of tired and it was a long week at work."

He nodded and went back to the kitchen. "Just lay there. I'll make you something to eat. Does an omelet sound okay or do you want something else?"

"You cook?" she asked, her voice loud with surprise.

He'd never actually done any cooking in the past when they'd been together, but he knew how to take care of basic things like breakfast and sandwiches. Anything more complicated than that and he'd need the takeout menu.

He checked her fridge and frowned. "You don't have anything in here."

"Yeah," she sighed. "I was supposed to go food shopping today."

PENNY SNEEZED AGAIN. She'd felt run down the previous day and should have known the cold was coming, but with everything that went on at the stupid bachelorette auction, she'd ignored her body's warning signs.

She peeked over the back of the sofa to the kitchen. Ethan searched through her fridge. He shut the door and returned to the living room. "I'm going to get some things to make breakfast. Got any requests?"

She nodded. "There's this bakery down the road that makes amazing croissants."

"I know which one. I used to get honey buns there. They're great." He marched out of the house, leaving her all kinds of confused.

Ethan, this Ethan, was so…different. The same, but different. There hadn't been this much catering to her when they'd been together before. In the past she'd felt like he'd been tiptoeing around her, almost afraid to say or do something to upset her.

The ringing of a cell phone caught her attention. She glanced at the coffee table. It was his phone. She shouldn't answer it, but curiosity had her staring at the screen. The name displayed didn't look familiar. She wouldn't answer. That was wrong and totally inappropriate. Besides, if it were her phone? She wouldn't want anyone answering her calls. The ringing stopped and the cell phone vibrated in her hand. She glanced down at the screen when a text message appeared.

Have you figured out what to do about your wife?

She blinked and re-read the message. Wife? Wife? Wife! Anger flourished inside her, growing into a massive monster looking for destruction. She took deep breaths and tried to ignore the pain. Ethan, married? Could it be? But why pursue her then? She shook her head and pushed the flood of emotions back. This could all be a misunderstanding. Ethan wasn't a cheater. Not that she was in a relationship with him, but she knew that much about him. She knew he wouldn't do that.

After ten minutes of pacing the living room until she couldn't stand her own inability to shut out the angry words springing to mind, she heard her door open.

"Sorry I took so long, I got the croissants and some other things to make breakfast," he said carrying large bags toward the kitchen.

"Your phone was ringing while you were gone. You forgot it on my table," she said, bringing it to the kitchen and handing it to him. Then she stood there, watching his face as he glanced at the screen, looking for any sign of guilt or fear.

He grinned and lifted his gaze from the phone. "Guess you're wondering about the text, huh?"

She shrugged as if it were no big deal. Like she wasn't visualizing ways to smash the phone on his head. "Oh? What message?"

He laughed and yanked her by her robe into his arms. "Will you believe me if I tell you I'm not married and you're the only woman I want?"

She thought about it for a second before replying. "Yes."

He hugged her tight and brushed his lips over her forehead. "I'm not married, I swear."

"I believe you. But why did you get a message asking about your wife?"

He let go of her and started taking food out of the bags. "That's my cousin Terry. She likes joking around because she knows you are the only woman I ever wanted for a wife. She'd heard about what I was doing at the auction and this was her way of asking how things went. When I met you, I told her you were going to be my wife, so she's been referring to you that way since then."

She frowned. "Wait, you told her I was going to be your wife since you met me?"

He nodded, placing the makings for breakfast on the counter. "Yes. From the very first day I knew you were it for me."

She gulped back the knot in her throat and sniffled. Stupid runny nose. Yeah, blame that and not the abundance of emotions filling her heart. "You...you never told me that."

He cupped her face with both hands; his honest gaze warmed her to the bone. "I didn't know how much I could give you back then. I didn't want to scare you. Bears know their mates. We live for them and don't ever want them away from us. That's the animal in me. The man loves the beauty he saw in you. The sweetness. The unselfishness. You're everything I could have asked for in a woman, Penny. Everything and more."

He'd really brought out the big guns. She wasn't sure if it was the fact that she had a cold or that she'd spent the entire night rehashing her feelings for Ethan, but she couldn't turn away from him. There was no leaving and not without giving them a second chance.

"Now, go lay down and let me pamper you."

Eight

SHE WENT BACK to the sofa and lay there with a throw over her. After dozing for a few minutes, she woke to the scent of food. She sat up when he came around the sofa with a tray. He put the tray on the table. He passed her a mug of tea with honey and lemon, and a plate of food.

"Wow, this looks so good. You didn't have to."

He winked. "Don't say that until you've tried it. You might be saying it for real after you eat."

She picked up a fork and ate, watching him drink a cup of coffee. The rest of the day went on like that, with him bringing things to her in bed and finally running a bath so she could lay down feeling refreshed. She took some cold medicine and woke up hours later to find him lying next to her. The idea of him and her again didn't bring on the fear and distress it once had. She'd been stupid and naïve. She should have trusted her instincts when it came to him.

He'd offered nothing but happiness and she'd blown it the moment she found out something he hadn't told her. Instead of getting angry, what she should have done was try to figure out why he'd felt the need to keep things from her. That would have saved her being away from her bear for a year: a year of loneliness and heartache.

She glanced at his face. Even in sleep he looked ready to break something. Her gaze caressed the beard growth on his chin. She continued letting her vision travel down. His chest rose and fell with smooth breaths. At the beginning of their relationship, she'd refused to believe she'd fallen for him so quickly. But she had.

After meeting him at a wild life conservation dinner, he didn't have to work too hard at getting her into his bed. From the moment their gazes clashed, lust and need exploded inside her. He'd done that. Taken her from a woman who never slept with a guy on a first date, to one who moved in with him a week later.

The passion between them hadn't dimmed the entire time they'd been together. Looking at him now, her body heating from just gazing at him, she knew the need for him would never go away. She moved down to his waist, unbuckled his jeans and shoved her hand in to grasp his cock, pumping him in her grip.

His eyes snapped open and his hand caught her wrist. "What are you doing?"

She grinned, her body humming with need. "If you have to ask, then I must not be doing something right."

He let go of her hand and she tugged his jeans down, until his erection was freed from the confines of the denim. She leaned forward and circled her tongue on the head of his cock, moaning at the salty taste of his smooth, velvety flesh.

She closed her eyes, her focus solely on him, making this moment good for both of them. With one hand, she pumped his shaft while pushing him further down her throat. He sucked in his abs with every scratch she did made down his chest.

He groaned, slid a fist into her hair and held on to a chunk. "That's fucking perfect, baby. I love how you suck my cock." He pushed her head toward his pelvis. "Those sexy sounds you make every time you suck are driving me crazy."

She knew what sounds he referred to. It was the saliva in her mouth combined with every slide of her lips over his slick dick. She scraped her nails on his abs with each hard suck.

"Take my cock, baby. Yeah," he grunted. "Fucking hell your mouth is so good. I can't fucking think straight."

She continued bobbing her head up and down his cock, jerking him with her hand. He tugged on the hair he had in his grip and let out a slow breath. "Come here. I want to taste that sweet honey coating your pussy."

She let go of his cock and sat back, taking off the tank top and short she'd had on. He didn't give her a second. He shoved her on to her back and curled his arms around her thighs, pushing her legs wide open and taking an immediate lick of her pussy. She squealed, her back coming off the bed and her fingers darting into his hair, to hold him in place.

"Oh, Ethan."

He shoved his tongue into her pussy, licking and suckling and making slurping noises she found so damn sexy. He kissed her inner thigh and then bit her. "I love your taste. I could live right here, fucking this sweet pussy with my tongue."

She opened her mouth and the only thing that came out was a loud moan. He lay his tongue flat on her pussy and swiped it up and down. Then, when she was squirming and rocking her hips hard on his face, he sucked her clit into his mouth, at first bypassing it with his tongue. Every small swipe made her muscles tense harder, until her legs were shaking and she was taking choppy breaths.

"Ethan, please."

He chuckled and licked another circle around her clit. "I fucking love you like this. Wet. Hungry. Ready to come all over my face."

"Stop the torture," she gasped.

Quick as lightning, he struck. He nibbled on her aching clit and sucked her hard. Her body shook as a wave of pleasure drained the tension away, bathing her in a sea of bliss.

She gasped, moaned and let her body do its own thing. She'd yet to catch a breath when he pushed his cock into her, her pussy walls still fluttering around him from her orgasm. He slid right in, taking her in a single drive.

He held her face in his hands, meeting her gaze with a tender one of his own. "I love you, Penny."

She hadn't wanted to think about love just yet, but there was no denying her feelings. She'd never stopped loving her bear.

"I love you too."

He pulled his hips back and drove forth, grunting with the punishing drive.

She whimpered, raking her nails over his large shoulders.

"I love your smile." He propelled back and pushed hard again. "I love every gorgeous curve on you. And don't you dare debate with me about how big you are. You're the perfect size for me."

She grinned. "I'm still really big."

"I like big. I love curves. Yours feel fucking amazing when I'm in you." He stroked his lips over hers. "More than anything, I don't want you to ever feel like I'm being dishonest or keeping things from you. I'll tell you everything. All I am is yours. All I own is yours." He kissed her harder, flirting his tongue over hers and then cutting the kiss short right when she opened up for more. "I don't feel whole unless you're with me."

"Please," she mumbled. "You have to move faster. I'm so close."

He thrust deeper. Every plunge pushed her to moan louder. To take sharper breaths. Everything but the feel of him possessing her body blurred. Nothing else mattered.

He gripped her hip with a hand, his fingers biting deep into her flesh. He rolled his own and she saw stars. His cock rubbed against an area that sent her soaring. The scream that rolled out of her caught her unawares. Her fingers turned stiff from how hard she clung to his shoulders. Her pussy clamped tight around his cock as pleasure washed over her, liquefying her bones and muscles.

His thrust turned jerky, every move slowed until he held stiff above her. Then he groaned, his cock filling her pussy with his cum. She gulped, trying to catch a breath. He flipped on his side, pulling her to lay sprawled half-on half-off him.

It took long minutes before either could move and when one did, it was her. She lifted her head from his chest to stare deep into his eyes.

"I love you. I don't want to be separated any longer."

"Thank fuck, baby. I don't think I could have survived it," he said, running his fingers over the back of her head. "I meant what I said. I won't ever keep anything from you again. You're the only woman I have ever loved and I don't ever want you to feel like I've deceived you in any way."

She smiled and laid her head back on his chest. "Good. Next time I won't be as nice."

"There won't be a next time. There's a forever and that's you and me, babe."

She liked the sound of that. Forever with her bear.

the end

about the author

New York Times and USA Today Bestselling Author Milly Taiden (AKA April Angel) loves to write sexy stories. How sexy? So sexy they will surely make your ereader sizzle. Usually paranormal or contemporary, her stories are a great quick way to satisfy your craving for fun heroines with curves and sexy alphas with fur.

Milly lives in New York City with her hubby, their boy child and their little dog "Needy Speedy." She's aware she's bossy and is addicted to shoe shopping, chocolate (but who isn't, right?), and Dunkin' Donuts coffee.

She loves to meet new readers!
Sign up for Milly's newsletter for latest news!
http://eepurl.com/pt9q1

FIND OUT MORE ABOUT MILLY TAIDEN HERE:

Email: millytaiden@gmail.com
Website: http://www.millytaiden.com
Facebook: http://www.facebook.com/millytaidenpage
Twitter: https://www.twitter.com/millytaiden

IF YOU LIKED THIS STORY, YOU MIGHT ALSO ENJOY BY MILLY TAIDEN:

Sassy Mates Series
Scent of a Mate *Sassy Mates Book One*
A Mate's Bite *Sassy Mates Book Two*
Unexpectedly Mated *Sassy Mates Book Three*
A Sassy Wedding *Short 3.7*
The Mate Challenge *Sassy Mates Book Four*
Sassy in Diapers *Short 4.3*

Federal Paranormal Unit
Wolf Protector *Federal Paranormal Unit Book One*
Dangerous Protector *Federal Paranormal Unit Book Two*

Black Meadow Pack
Sharp Change *Black Meadows Pack Book One*
Caged Heat *Black Meadows Pack Book Two*

Paranormal Dating Agency

Twice the Growl *Book One*

Geek Bearing Gifts *Book Two*

The Purrfect Match *Book Three*

Curves 'Em Right *Book Four*

Tall, Dark and Panther *Book Five (coming soon)*

FUR-ocious Lust

Fur-Bidden *Book One*

Fur-Gotten *Book Two (March)*

Fur-Given Book *Three (April)*

Other Works

Wolf Fever *Alpha Project Book One*

Fate's Wish

Wynter's Captive

Sinfully Naughty Vol. 1

Club Duo Boxed Set

Don't Drink and Hex

Hex Gone Wild

Hex and Kisses

Hex You Up *(coming soon)*

Hex with an Ex *(coming soon)*

Alpha Owned

Bitten by Night

Seduced by Days

Mated by Night
Taken by Night
Captured by Night *(coming soon)*
Match Made in Hell *(coming soon)*
Hellhound Needs a Mate *(coming soon)*

If you enjoyed the book, please consider leaving a review, even if it's only a line or two; it would make all the difference and would be very much appreciated.

Thank you!

Made in the USA
San Bernardino, CA
25 April 2015